I wish I could...

Buzz with the BUGS

Written by Gordy Slack
Illustrated by C. Buck Reynolds

Dr. David Kavanaugh, scientific advisor

Roberts Rinehart Publishers
in cooperation with

CALIFORNIA
ACADEMY
OF
SCIENCES ™
GOLDEN GATE PARK

For Jonah, my bee all and ent. all—G.S.
For Ryan, the project's chief bug catcher—C.B.R.

Published by Roberts Rinehart Publishers
6309 Monarch Park Place
Niwot, Colorado 80503
Tel 303.652.2685
Fax 303.652.2689
www.robertsrinehart.com

In cooperation with the California Academy of Sciences
Golden Gate Park
San Francisco, California 94118

Distributed to the trade by Publishers Group West

Published in Ireland and the UK by
Roberts Rinehart Publishers
Trinity House, Charleston Road
Dublin 6, Ireland

Library of Congress Cataloging-in-Publication Data
Slack, Gordy.
    I wish I could—buzz with the bugs / written by Gordy Slack   ;
illustrated by C. Buck Reynolds.
        p.   cm.
    Summary: A brother and sister enter the world of insects, where they learn
about such things as metomorphosis, insect anatomy, camouflage, and evolution.
    ISBN 1-57098-220-1 (sc)
    1. Insects—Miscellanea—Juvenile literature.   [1. Insects.]
I. Reynolds, C. Buck, ill. II. Title
QL467.2.S58   1998   98-24340
595.7—dc21   CIP
                                                 AC

Production: Cathy Holtz, Blonde Ambition
Printed in Hong Kong

These bugs are huge!
No, we're small. And those aren't insects. They're isopods called wood lice. See how many legs they have? Insects only have six.

That's right. A few other things can help tell
if something is an insect or not.

People have skeletons inside their bodies. But insects have skeletons
outside. Called exoskeletons, these outer shells hold insects together,
keep them from drying out, and protect them from predators.
        Because insects have exoskeletons, they must grow in a number
of distinct stages. Each stage requires breaking out of their old
exoskeleton and making a new one.

All insects have three main body parts:
        A head, where the brain and mouth parts are.
        A thorax, where the six legs and two sets of wings are.
        And an abdomen, where the digestive and
        reproductive organs are.

It's a silverfish!
I've seen these in our kitchen.

Scientists believe silverfish are a lot like the first insects on Earth. They're "living fossils" and look pretty much like some of the wingless insects that were around 350 million years ago.

Mantids are masters of disguise. Some look just like the flowers they stand on. Others resemble the leaves they hang out among. When an insect looks like its surroundings, it is camouflaged. Blending in like this makes it harder for predators to find and make a meal of you. Many insects, like this mantid, use their camouflage to help them catch a meal. This butterfly never saw what hit it.

Ah, now here's an insect!

A female dragonfly lays its eggs on plants in or near the water. When they hatch, the babies, called nymphs, live in the pond. Like fish, they have gills and can breathe underwater. When a nymph is ready, it climbs out of the water onto a reed, cracks out of its exoskeleton, stretches its wings, and flies into adulthood. Adults have been clocked flying 60 miles per hour!

Some insects spend their adult lives on or in the water, too. A water strider "skates" on the water's surface waiting for other insects to fall in, so it can catch and eat them.

Two of the diving beetle's legs have adapted into paddles it can use to row underwater. At the surface, the diving beetle traps an air bubble under its wing covers. It brings this bubble on its underwater travels like a SCUBA diver's air tank. Diving beetles hunt anything they can catch, including tiny fish, salamanders, and tadpoles.

Most female mosquitoes have tubular mouthparts
that can pierce animal skin. Most also need to drink blood
before they can develop fertile eggs. Like dentists injecting
Novocain before they drill, mosquitoes inject a pain killer
as they puncture an animal's skin so their prey doesn't feel
the bite.

Male mosquitoes have feathery antennae, which they use to
"listen" for females. Males don't bite.

There are about 115,000 species of bees and wasps. Most of these live alone or in simply organized groups, but some live in very complicated societies.

Beetles are probabl[y]
the most successful grou[p]
of insects, with at least 300,00[0]
different kinds. The front set of beetle[s']]
wings are hard covers, which shield their bodies.
The ladybird beetle (sometimes called a ladybug) tastes so ba[d]
most predators don't even try to eat it.

If insects were a little smarter, I bet they could take over the Earth.

They already did. Pound for pound there are more insects than any other kind of animal. Most insects would hardly notice it if people disappeared from the face of the Earth.

Ants are social and live in organized groups, called colonies. Some ants raid the nests of termites and other kinds of ants to eat their young. Another kind, called the slave-making ant, steals the pupae of a different species and makes slaves of the adults that emerge. The slave ants gather food and take care of the nest for the masters.

All animals get older, and aging always means changing. But because their skeletons are on the outside and do not stretch, each insect grows in one of two special ways. The first, called complete metamorphosis, is the way butterflies, bees, ants, beetles, and flies grow.

Complete metamorphosis has four different stages. First comes the egg. When it hatches, an insect breaks out, sometimes eating its own eggshell as its first meal. It then enters the second stage, called the larval stage. Caterpillars are larval butterflies and maggots are larval flies. Most insects do a lot of eating in their larval stage.

Eventually, the larva finds a safe place to burrow or to hang. Most insects, like butterflies, stop eating or drinking during this period and molt to a third, resting stage called the pupa. Some pupae are in protective cases called cocoons, which are made by the larva before it enters the pupa stage.

Eventually, the pupa's skin cracks open and, when the adult insect comes out, the fourth and final stage of life begins.

Some insects, like mantids and grasshoppers, undergo incomplete metamorphosis. They still have different stages of life. And they still have to break out of their exoskeletons, but the young look pretty much like the adults, except smaller. But only the adults have working wings.

About 10,000 new kinds, or species, of insects get discovered every year. There are probably several million insect species.

Insects live everywhere: in caves, on icy mountaintops, in the hottest deserts, even on and inside of people and other animals.

Insects are so successful partly because they are such good eaters. If something can be eaten, some insect probably eats it.

Most insects eat plants, but some eat insects, other animals (living and dead), and even animal droppings.

Dung beetles collect animal dung and mold it into balls. They roll these balls into underground tunnels, where they also lay their eggs. When their larvae hatch, they can begin feasting right away.

Is it true that female preying mantids sometimes eat their mates?

Sometimes. So far I've been able to stay out of that kind of relationship.

Yuck!

Almost all insects
have a set of eating tools,
called mouthparts. But since
insects eat such a wide variety of
foods, different species have
very different kinds
of mouthparts.

Mosquitoes have long, thin mouthparts
good for piercing skin and sucking blood.
Grasshopper mouthparts can cut and chew
plants. And some butterfly mouthparts are
good for sucking nectar from deep inside flowers.

The Sri Lankan ant is only 1/30 of an inch long.

The atlas moth is one of the world's largest insects. Its wingspan can be 12 inches across. Asian walking sticks can be more than 14 inches long.

Reproduction is essential for any animal, but insects go to amazing lengths to reproduce. The male luna moth, for instance, neither eats nor drinks during his entire adult life. His only concern is to find a female and mate before his three-day-long adulthood is over.

The female luna moth gives off a powerful chemical, called a pheromone. Males, equipped with huge, very sensitive antennae, can smell this pheromone from nearly three miles away.

A chemical reaction in fireflies causes a part of their abdomens to light up. This helps males and females find each other at night, when fewer predators are hunting.

All insects must be very sensitive to the environments they live in. Those that spend most of their time in the light of day, like dragonflies and horseflies, generally have compound eyes that help them sense movement. Dragonflies may have as many as 28,000 individual eyes, called ommatidia, in each compound eye.

Some crickets, grasshoppers, locusts, cicadas, and moths have organs on their legs or abdomens that sense vibrations the way eardrums do. This is about as close as insects come to hearing.

Hair-like bristles that protrude from an insect's exoskeleton can tell it a lot about the world outside. Some bristles on the wings of insects are so sensitive that a change in air movement can signal the approach of prey or predator.

Super-sensitive antennae give many insects lots of useful information about the taste, feel, smell, and temperature of the world around them.

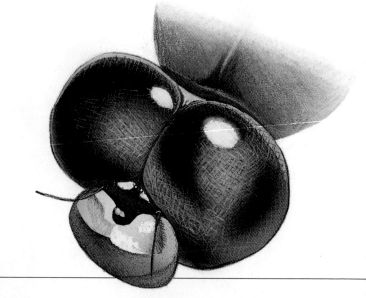

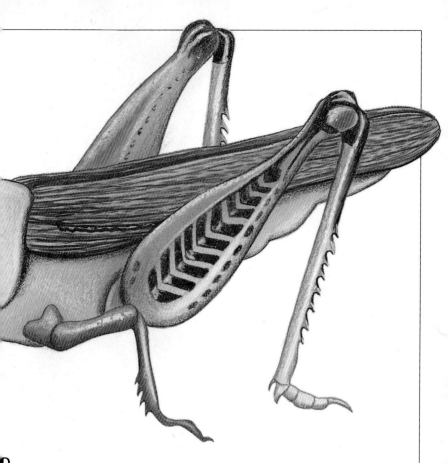

Because insects don't have voices, they find other ways to communicate. One way is to rub one part of their body against another. This is called stridulation. Grasshoppers, for instance, scrape the inner side of their leg against a thick vein on their forewing. It works something like a violin.

Social insects often need to communicate the location of a food source. Some bees can tell each other with dances where to go. Ants and other insects leave chemical trails, which others can follow.

All termites and ants, and some wasps and bees, live in organized communities. This gives them some big advantages. One, or a few, can concentrate on laying eggs, while others collect food, fight off enemies, take care of the young, or build nests.

Depending on their jobs, or castes, ants of the same species can look very different from one another. Queens are built for reproduction, and have abdomens that can hold many eggs.

A few ant species have soldiers with big jaws for fighting off threats to the colony. Because it is so specialized, no individual ant can survive long when separated from the group.

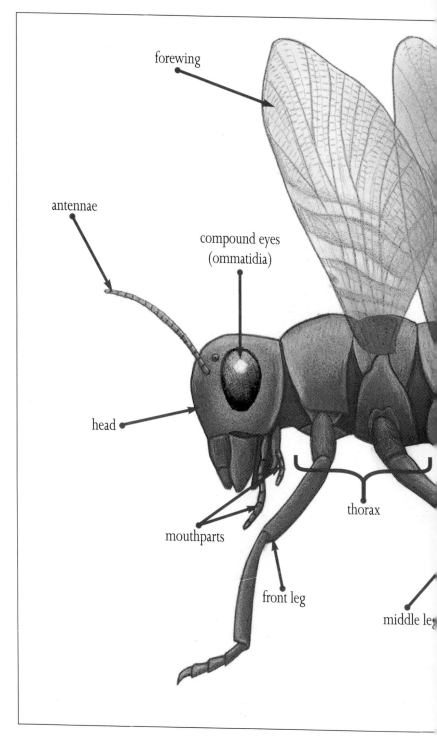

forewing

antennae

compound eyes
(ommatidia)

head

mouthparts

thorax

front leg

middle leg

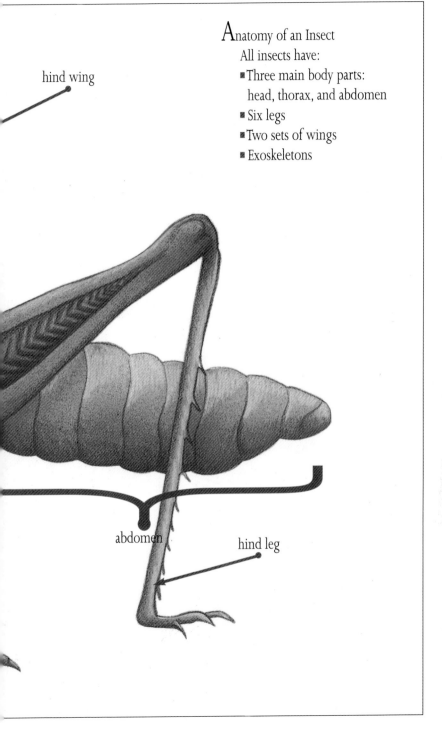

hind wing

Anatomy of an Insect
All insects have:
- Three main body parts: head, thorax, and abdomen
- Six legs
- Two sets of wings
- Exoskeletons

abdomen

hind leg

Leafcutter ants are farmers. They chew up leaves into a kind of mulch, which they bury in their nests. The mulch rots and grows a fungus on it. By tending the fungus, the ants make it blossom. These bulb-like blossoms are the ants' main food source.

A few species of ants take care of "flocks" of aphids (small insects that drink the sap of plants), which produce a sweet mixture of sugars called honeydew. An ant just needs to stroke an aphid with his antennae to make it release a drop of honeydew from its rear end. In exchange for this food the ants protect the aphids from predators.

All living things change a little with each generation. Over many generations these little changes add up to big ones. If an insect changes in a way that helps it get more food, say, or to protect itself, then its chances of surviving and reproducing improve. When it reproduces, the helpful trait is passed on to its offspring. This process is called natural selection.

Insects first evolved about 350 million years ago. Scientists know this because they have found fossils of early insects in rocks that old.

About 300 million years ago, there was a gigantic kind of dragonfly called Meganeura. It measured at least 2½ feet from wingtip to wingtip.

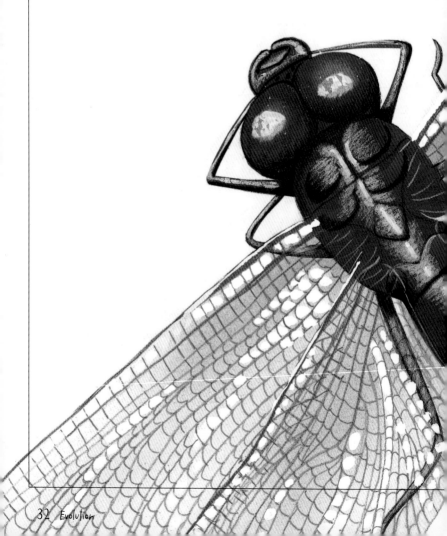

Since there are many ways to make a living, two separate populations of the same kind of insect might well change (evolve) in different ways. One population of a butterfly, say, might develop larger wings to fly further in search of food. Another population might develop smaller wings, to make it harder for predators to catch. This is one important way that new insect species evolve. But this kind of change is very gradual and takes a long time.

Kingdom = Animal
Phylum = Arthropoda
Class = Insecta
Order = Orthoptera
Family = Mantidae
Genus = Mantis
Species =

religiosa

Many insects have common names that people often use when talking abou them, such as mosquito, horsefly, and yellow jacket. But the same kind of insec may have several different names in English, let alone in the world's hundreds o other languages.

To avoid confusion, it's very important for scientists to have a precise way to refer to them. They do this with scientific names, which are usually in Latin, th language used by scientists in the 18th century. Scientific names also help describ the evolutionary relationship between different insects.

The simple scientific name for this preying mantid is *Mantis religiosa*, but its fu name, and the description of its place in the evolutionary family tree of life o Earth, is shown in this diagram.

Whatever you call them, insects do a lot of serious work that helps people.

Life without insects would be boring.

By eating and digesting dead animals and plants, insects recycle nutrients back into the earth and create new and healthy soil.

Insects carry pollen from one plant to another, allowing plants to reproduce. Farmers need insects to raise their crops.

Some insects, like ladybird beetles, eat aphids and other insects that, if left alone, would destroy crops.

Bees make honey and beeswax. And silkworm moth larvae make silk.

Glossary

abdomen: the third section of an insect, containing digestive and reproductive organs

antennae: sensory organs on the head

camouflage: an adaptation allowing an animal to look like its surroundings, so it is hard to see

cocoon: a structure that covers a developing pupa

colony: a group of social insects

common name: the informal name given to a species or group of insects

complete metamorphosis: metamorphosis that includes egg, pupal, larval, and adult stages

compound eyes: insect eyes made of numerous simple eyes, called the ommatidia

dung: excrement

exoskeleton: light and strong exterior skeleton of an insect

incomplete metamorphosis: metamorphosis that includes only egg, nymph, and adult stages

larvae: immature stages of insects that undergo complete metamorphosis

metamorphosis: the change in form during development of an insect

molting: when an insect sheds an exoskeleton in order to grow or metamorphose

nymphs: immature stages of insects that undergo incomplete metamorphosis

ommatidium: the individual eyes that together (plural: ommatidia) make up a compound eye

pollinator: animal that moves pollen from one plant to another, facilitating fertilization

predator: animal that lives by hunting and eating other animals

prey: animal hunted and eaten by other animals

pupa: in insects that undergo complete metamorphosis, the resting stage following the larval stage, from which the adult insect emerges (plural: pupae)

scientific name: the unique name used by scientists to identify precisely a kind of organism

species: a unique kind of organism

stridulate: rubbing one part of the body against another to produce a sound

thorax: middle part of an insect's body, containing the legs and wings